Nola The Nurse® & her Super Friends

learn about Mardi Gras safety

Holiday Series

COLORING BOOK

by Dr. Scharmaine Lawson, NP.

illustrated by Marvin Alonso

Nola The Nurse® & her Super Friends: learn about Mardi Gras Safety Coloring Book

A DrNurse Publishing House, New Orleans, Louisiana

Text copyright © 2023 by Dr. Scharmaine Lawson

ISBN:
Paperback 978-1-945088-54-4

For information address A DrNurse Publishing House®
7041 Canal Blvd., #125, New Orleans, La. 70124
www.DrLawsonNP.com
Author Contact info: DrLawson@DrLawsonNP.com
www.NolaTheNurse.com

Dedication

Dear Skylar & Wyatt, my S1S2. Mommy loves you more than life itself! Thank you for giving me the space to dream, create, and make memories with the two of you.

Fat
Tuesday

N NURS

Fat
Tuesday

18

22

Nola
The Nurse ®

Bax The Nurse®

Maddi The Midwife®

Charo
The CRNA®

Gumbo

More books by *Dr. Scharmaine Lawson*

Fiction

- Nola The Nurse®, She's On The Go Series Vol 1 (available in Spanish and French)
- Nola The Nurse® & Friends Explore The Holi Fest, She's On The Go Series Vol 2
- Nola The Nurse® & Friends Explore The Holi Fest, She's On The Go Series Vol 2 coloring book
- Nola The Nurse® & Bax Join The Protest
- Nola the Nurse & Bax Join The Protest coloring book
- Nola The Nurse® Activity Book for Preschool Vol 1
- Nola The Nurse® Activity Book for Kindergarten Vol 2
- Nola The Nurse® Math Worksheets for Kindergarten Vol 3
- Nola The Nurse® English/Sight Worksheets for Kindergarten Vol 4
- Nola The Nurse® Math/English Worksheets for Preschoolers Vol 5
- Nola The Nurse® Math Worksheets for First Graders Vol 6
- Nola The Nurse® STEM Activity Book for 5-8-year-olds Vol 7
- Nola The Nurse® & Friends Explore The Holi Fest She's On The Go Series Vol 2
- Nola The Nurse® & Friends Explore The Holi Fest She's On The Go Series Vol 2 Coloring Book
- Nola The Nurse® Remembers Hurricane Katrina Special Edition
- Nola The Nurse® Remembers Hurricane Katrina Special Edition Coloring Book
- Nola The Nurse®: Let's Talk About Germs, The Germy series, Vol. 1
- Nola The Nurse®: Let's Talk About Germs, The Germy series, Vol. 1 coloring book
- Nola The Nurse® How To Stop Those Yuck Germs, The Germy series, Vol 2
- Nola The Nurse® How To Stop Those Yuck Germs, The Germy series, Vol 2 coloring book
- Nola The Nurse® & her Super Friends Learn About Mardi Gras Safety, Holiday series, Vol 1
- Nola The Nurse® & her Super Friends Learn About Mardi Gras Safety, Holiday series, Vol 1 coloring book
- Nola The Nurse® Cursive Handwriting Workbook For Kids
- Nola The Nurse® Science Word & Puzzle Search For Kids
- Nola The Nurse® Mandala Coloring Book for kids
- Nola The Nurse® Coloring Book for Kids
- Black Dot

Non-Fiction

- Housecalls 101: The only book you will ever need to begin your medical practice, Part I
- Housecalls 101: A Clinician's Guide To In-Home Health Care, Telemedicine Services, and Long-Distance Treatment For a Post-Pandemic World, Part II
- Housecalls 101 Policy & Procedure Manual
- Culture Stories: Racism, Bias, and Prejudice in Nursing (soon to be released)
- Pandemic Parenting
- The Business of Nur$ing: The Blueprint

www.NolaTheNurse.com

www.DrLawsonNP.com

Podcast

Nite Nite Nurse Podcast

https://open.spotify.com/show/3nGnfpXTUfVUx2mQTrsWrG?si=1881e7a2728545fe

DrLawson@DrLawsonNP.com